Wish Fish

Book 2
Endless Possibilities

*AN EXCITING ADVENTURE
OF POSSIBILITIES*

LYNN MICLEA

Wish Fish

Book 2

*The Incredible Wish Fish Adventure
Continues...*

ISBN-10: 153504926X
ISBN-13: 978-1535049269
CreateSpace Independent Publishing Platform
North Charleston, South Carolina

DEDICATION

୨ ୧

This is dedicated to all of you who want to be the best that you can, and have wondered how far you can go.

To anyone who has had fears, self-doubts, or insecurities – please know that you are an amazing, incredible person, filled with unique and extraordinary gifts, and for all of you, the possibilities are truly endless.

This book is for you.

TABLE OF CONTENTS

INTRODUCTION

"Wish Fish Book 2" takes off where *"Wish Fish Book 1"* left off. In this story, Ray and Roxy help other fish, face incredible new danger, break through previously-imagined limitations, learn from a Master, perform amazing feats, and unleash their true inner joy. And, in the process, they discover that the real possibilities are astoundingly endless.

Join these two sweet fish friends in this uplifting, loving, feel-good story, as they realize that they have become so much more than they could have imagined. It becomes clear that there are boundless possibilities to what they can achieve and become.

This is a beautiful and empowering story, filled with warm humor, which helps all of us learn to not hold ourselves back by outdated thoughts, fears, and perceived limitations, but to open and find that we really are so much more than we thought we could be.

The author believes that all of us have incredible depth and potential, and we are so much more than we think we are. Too many of us tend to hold ourselves back from our full potential due to fears, doubts, insecurities, and perceived limitations. It is time to break free from all of that, and through this book, the author hopes to help people discover that all of us are amazing, joyful, and incredible beings, filled with extraordinary gifts.

It is important for each of us to be empowered, to believe in ourselves, and to have confidence in our gifts and abilities in order to become more than we can possibly imagine.

We need to deeply love and cherish who we are. Each of us is naturally filled with so much love and joy, and by believing in ourselves, we can help change the world by sharing that love and joy with others. And when we do that, the possibilities are truly endless.

Don't miss out – If you have not yet read the first book in this series – get *"Wish Fish Book 1 – Discovering the Secret."*

This first book is where the story began with the same two Wish Fish. Find out how they started, faced their fears and self-doubts, discovered that they are Wish Fish, and learned the secret behind being a Wish Fish.

If you don't already have it, get your copy today!

❧ CHAPTER 1 ☙
Helping Bella

Rain pounded on the surface of the ocean, making the water darker than usual.

"Roxy," Ray said, turning toward his sweet friend. "We need to go back to more shallow water. I don't like being out here where it's so deep. It's getting darker, and we need to stay out of danger."

"Oh, Ray," Roxy laughed. "You are always so worried. You need to lighten up." She wiggled her golden-yellow fins playfully. "Try and catch me!"

Ray watched her swim off into the murky depths, and he had no choice but to go after her. He loved her more than anything. She could make him smile like no other fish ever could. He adored her, and being around her was always so much fun.

He could swim faster than Roxy, and Ray easily caught up to her. She was hiding behind a large rock, but a quick glimpse of yellow caught his eye, and he knew that was her.

"Ha!" Ray said as he swam up to her, his golden-yellow body matching hers. "I found you. Now let's go back where it's safer. We're just little fish, and it's dangerous out here."

"Okay, that's fine with me. It's harder to see now since the water is getting darker," Roxy answered him in her sweet little fish voice, as she swished her tail.

They swam back toward a calmer and lighter area, passing other bigger fish, which made tremors of fear pass through them. As they got closer to home, they relaxed a bit more.

Sudden waves and splashing off to one side got their attention. *What was that?*

They turned to see two bright red fish with black tails frantically turning in circles.

"What's wrong?" Ray asked them.

"We can't find our baby," one of them answered. "I don't know where she went."

"We can help you look," Roxy offered.

Ray and Roxy started swimming in slow circles around the area, looking behind rocks and seaweed.

A sudden flash of brilliant red caught Ray's eye. *"There!"* he shouted.

He and Roxy swam toward it. They found hidden there, behind a soft green fern, was a small, crying, baby red fish.

"Hi, Sweetie," Roxy said to the little red fish, reaching out to comfort her. "Are you okay? Are you lost?"

"I can't find my mommy," the little red fish cried, her fins quivering.

"We know where your mommy is. Come with us. We'll take you back to her."

"I'm scared," the little red fish wailed.

"We understand," Ray told her gently. "We won't hurt you. Stay with us, close to our side, and we will protect you as we take you back to your mommy and daddy."

"Okay," the little red fish sniffed.

"What's your name?" Roxy asked her.

"Bella," the little fish answered softly.

"What a pretty name!" Roxy said. "Bella, stay with us, and we will keep you safe."

"Your mommy is not far away," Ray added.

Bella nodded, and the three of them swam back to where the bigger red fish were. The bigger fish were still frantically looking around, turning in all directions.

"Bella, is that your mommy and daddy?" Roxy asked, pointing with her fin.

"Mommy!" cried Bella happily.

The two bigger red fish turned toward the sound and immediately rushed over. "Bella!" They cried. "We were so worried about you! You can't run off like that. We didn't know where you were or what happened."

They hugged and swam around each other over and over in a flurry of excited, red movement.

"I'm sorry, I was just playing and then I didn't know where I was," Bella said in a soft baby voice.

The two parent fish swarmed all around Bella, relief and happiness showing in their faces.

"Thank you," they called out to Ray and Roxy, swishing their tails in gratitude.

"We're happy that we found her," Ray answered.

"And that she's home and safe now," Roxy added, smiling.

They waved their fins, as they turned and continued toward their home in more shallow water.

"I'm so glad we reunited Bella with her parents," Roxy said.

"Me, too," Ray said, "I was really worried for them. And that's why I don't like it when *you* run off. You could get hurt or lost or worse."

"But I'm not a baby," Roxy said.

"I know, but you never know what can happen out there. Sometimes the ocean can be a terrifying place."

"Well, I'm okay now. And look, it stopped raining."

They looked around and saw streaks of sunlight breaking through the water around them. It was beautiful and warm, and the green ferns were glowing in the soft golden rays of the sun.

Ray loved living there in the ocean. And he especially liked living there with Roxy. There were so many things to see and do, and sharing it all with her made everything even better.

Ϩ CHAPTER 2 ℓ
Can Fish Sing?

Where did Roxy go this time? She could be very playful, and Ray wanted to keep an eye on her. He swam around looking for her, slightly worried.

He swam around a few rocks, behind some seaweed, and then Ray caught sight of yellow behind a fern. He knew right away that it was Roxy. He swam up to her and heard a humming sound.

"Roxy?"

"What?" She jumped, a bit startled, and the humming stopped.

"Were you singing?" Ray asked, astonished.

"No, silly, fish can't sing." Roxy rolled her eyes.

"But I heard you – you were humming. It was pretty."

"Really?"

"Yes, it was. You have a nice voice. And I want to sing, too."

"Oh, that is nuts. Fish can't sing, silly."

"Do again what you were just doing."

Roxy started humming, "Mmmmmmm-hmmmmmm..."

Ray gulped a mouthful of water and loudly joined her. "Lala, lalala..."

"Ack!" Roxy shouted, startled. "What was that?"

"I was singing with you."

"I don't think so. It sounded like you were in pain," Roxy teased. She smiled and snorted.

"Ha," Ray laughed. "I bet I sounded great."

Roxy snorted again and bubbles rose from her nose. "That was not so good, Ray. See, there's a reason fish don't sing. Even Wish Fish can't sing."

"Hey, I was singing harmony."

"That was agony, not harmony," Roxy said laughing and rolling her eyes again.

"But we're Wish Fish, and Wish Fish can do anything."

"Well, maybe even Wish Fish have their limits," Roxy retorted.

"Okay, I'll practice more before we try again."

"Practice quietly. Or maybe in a cave where no one can hear you," Roxy added, giggling. "We don't want to get a ticket for disturbing the peace."

"Hey, Wish Fish can sing. Maybe we can even dance."

"Fish can't dance, you silly thing. That's absurd."

"Sure we can – we can do the Wish-Fish Cha-Cha. Here, take my fin," Ray instructed, as he reached for Roxy's small yellow fin. "Now follow me," he said, as he pulled Roxy closer and tried to spin her around.

Roxy moved sideways and bumped her nose into Ray.

Ray laughed and bubbles rose up from his mouth.

"That was actually fun," Roxy giggled.

Ray reached for her fin again, and Roxy twirled, flowing and spinning, her golden scales glistening as she moved. He twirled her one more time, and she was a little off-balance.

"Ooops!" Roxy said, "That was really fun, but I need more practice at this. Then we can try again. But in the meantime, bet you can't catch me!" And she took off around a clump of seaweed.

Ray had no choice but to chase after her again. She was spontaneous and playful, and sometimes more than he could handle, but he knew that he really loved her, and he would do anything to make her happy.

❧ CHAPTER 3 ❧
It's Raining Rocks

Ray swam after Roxy, following her trail of bubbles. She darted around a rock, and Ray chased after her. They swam around some ferns and seaweed, enjoying the feel of the cool, silky water.

PLOP!

"What was that?" Ray gasped, startled, as he both heard and felt the vibrations in the water.

They looked around as another rock suddenly sunk through the water next to them. *PLOP!* The tremors from the rock spread through the water.

"Huh?" Roxy looked at Ray, her eyes wide with fear.

PLOP! Another rock landed in the water near them, even closer this time. *How could this be? How could rocks fall from the sky?*

Ray swam up to the surface of the ocean for a better view. Looking up at the sky, he saw nothing. Then he looked toward the sandy shore.

On the shore he saw two small land creatures, two boys, laughing, shouting, and throwing rocks toward them. *Rocks that could hurt or even kill them!*

He quickly dove back down to tell Roxy.

"What is it?" Roxy asked, as another rock plummeted through the water inches away from them. *PLOP!*

"We need to get out of here *fast.* There are small land creatures throwing rocks at us."

"Oh, no!" Roxy turned to swim away, but then suddenly stopped. "Wait – look over there. I can see seahorses over there that are also in danger. We have to help them get away, too!"

"There's no time," Ray told her.

"It doesn't matter. We can't leave them here. What if they get hurt?" she said, while swimming toward the four black-and-white fish huddling behind a big rock.

PLOP! Another rock fell between her and the seahorses.

"Hey!" Roxy called out to the seahorses, as Ray scrambled after her and quickly reached them.

The four black-and-white fish were clustered together, shaking with fear. They looked at Roxy but did not respond.

"You guys need to move," Ray told them.

"There are rocks raining down on us," Roxy explained.

PLOP! This rock fell only inches away from them.

"We are not good swimmers," one of them said.

"You'll be out of danger if you move away – follow us," Ray told them.

They started swimming farther away from the shore, and the four seahorses lurched slowly after them. They wiggled their fins, but they did not move fast.

"This way," Roxy yelled, as she moved into deeper water, while another rock landed in the water where they had just been.

Ray and Roxy swam around the four seahorses, who were moving as quickly as they could. The water got deeper and darker. After a while, they did not hear any more rocks. *Were they okay now?*

"Wow," Roxy said, after a few minutes without hearing any other rocks. "I'm glad we got away from there."

"Yes, we could easily have been hurt," one of the seahorses said. "You really helped us. We didn't know what to do."

"That's right, we don't swim very well," another seahorse said, "and we didn't know where to go. You saved us!"

"You're out of danger now," Ray told them. "Don't go too close to the shore. There are small land creatures throwing rocks into the ocean, but they can't reach this far out."

"Land creatures? *Those are real?*" asked one of the seahorses, with his eyes wide with fear.

"Yes, we saw them," Ray told them.

"Thank you for helping us," another seahorse said, a tremor in his voice. "We are in your debt."

"We are happy that we could help you. Stay safe now," Roxy told them.

The four seahorses waved good-bye and headed into some nearby ferns for protection.

"I'm really glad we were able to get them to a safer area," Ray said.

"That was scary," Roxy said. "We got them out of there just in time." A shudder went through her yellow body.

"Let's swim around here for a while," Ray told her.

They passed the ferns where the black-and-white seahorses were huddled, swam around a rock, and then slowly glided through the cool water.

"Let's fly again," Ray said after they had rested.

"I can't get used to that. It still seems like fish shouldn't be able to fly," Roxy answered him.

"But *we* can. We're Wish Fish," Ray stated. "You have to believe in yourself."

"It's still hard for me to believe that we can fly. We're just fish."

"I know. But I'm learning that as a Wish Fish, we can do lots of things. More than we thought we could," Ray answered. "I bet there's even things we can do that we don't know yet."

"Maybe," Roxy replied. "But we're still just little fish."

"But remember the secret? We're more than we think we are."

"I'm still not sure about that," Roxy said. "But maybe we can practice dancing again," she added with a giggle.

Ray smiled at her, and as he reached for her fin, Roxy suddenly gasped, a look of terror on her face.

"What?" Ray asked, as his eyes quickly searched the area.

"Ray, look out!" Roxy suddenly yelled, pointing behind him.

Ray turned around and saw a huge, dark fish coming right at him. His eyes got big, as fear shot through his body.

No! It was too late to get away!

⧼ Chapter 4 ⧽
Don't Eat Me!

"I'm invisible, I'm invisible," Ray desperately shouted.

"HELP!" Roxy yelled, but it was too late. Before they could move or swim or become invisible, the big fish was upon them. Ray saw a huge mouth open, lined with sharp, white teeth, and then everything got dark.

It was hot and dark and Ray couldn't see a thing. *Now what?*

"Roxy?" Ray's voice said, quivering with fear.

"I'm here," she answered softly, her voice shaky.

"I can't see anything," he said desperately, in a small fish voice.

"What can we do?"

"Maybe we can glow so we can see a little bit," Ray said.

"Fish can't glow, Ray," Roxy retorted.

"Well, we were able to change color and also become invisible. So if we could do that, then maybe we can glow."

"That's ridiculous," Roxy said and snorted, despite her fear.

"Do you have a better idea?" Ray asked her.

Roxy didn't respond.

"Glow, Roxy. We can glow," Ray stated, remembering how they had changed colors. And he began to radiate a soft light around him.

"I can glow," Roxy responded, and within moments, Ray could see her. There was a soft, glowing light surrounding her.

"We can glow!" Ray repeated, feeling more confident. The amount of light around them increased.

There was now enough light to look around and see that they were, indeed, in the mouth of the big fish. They could see rows of white, angled, sharp teeth surrounding them.

"We need to get this fish to open its mouth," Ray said, fear filling his voice.

"How? That's impossible," Roxy answered, her voice still shaky. She tried to snort again, but a strange strangled sound came out.

"I don't know. Big fish, open your mouth," he said.

Nothing happened, and Roxy rolled her eyes.

"Big fish, you are sleepy," Ray suddenly chanted. "You are very tired."

"Yes, you are sleepy," Roxy repeated, catching on.

"It's your bed time," Ray added.

"Time for a nap," said Roxy. "You want to yawn."

Ray and Roxy looked at each other in the dim, glowing light. *Would this work?*

Suddenly, Ray felt panic and terror flood through his body, as it felt like they were being pulled toward the back of the fish's throat.

No! Could they get the fish to open its mouth in time?

Then they saw a sliver of light begin to appear between the rows of teeth, and they could see the ocean beyond. *The big fish was beginning to open its mouth!*

The view slowly grew bigger. *It was working! The big fish was yawning!* Within seconds, the big fish jaws slowly opened into a huge yawn.

"Swim!" yelled Ray, frantic.

"Let's go!" yelled Roxy, desperate to get out.

They swam as fast as their little bodies could, out of the mouth of the big fish, and into the cool ocean. *They were free!*

They turned back to quickly glance behind them, and they saw the big fish close its mouth and look around, confused. It suddenly saw the two of them, and it realized that its lunch was getting away.

As the big fish now surged toward them, Ray felt his body shake, as panic took over.

"Fly! We can fly!" Ray yelled.

"We can fly!" Roxy yelled back.

The two little yellow fish flew out of the water in a small arc, landing a short distance away. The big fish searched the water, looking for them.

"We're invisible!" Ray yelled.

"We're invisible!" Roxy repeated.

The big fish, losing sight of the tasty lunch he had wanted, gave up. He swam in a different direction, looking for other fish that would be easier to catch.

"Whew, that was close," Ray said, as his body returned to a natural and visible yellow.

"Too close," Roxy nodded, still trembling, as her body also came back into view, with beautiful yellow scales.

"I'm glad we got away," Ray said.

"I didn't know we could glow like that," Roxy told him, a slight tremor still in her voice.

"I didn't know either," Ray responded. "But we're Wish Fish. And we're learning new tricks. We can do anything we want."

"I just want to be safe," Roxy muttered quietly.

"And I want to keep you happy and safe," Ray said. "Let's go back to more shallow water where it's much quieter."

He wanted to protect Roxy more than anything. She was the sweetest and most beautiful fish he ever knew.

Ray circled around Roxy, as she looked at him, her eyes still filled with fear.

"I agree, let's get out of the deep water," Roxy told him.

They slowly swam back toward more shallow water, where it was warmer and calmer.

❧ CHAPTER 5 ❧
Having Doubts

After resting in calmer water for a while, Ray and Roxy finally felt more relaxed. They swam slowly, staying in the shallow area for a bit.

"Let's explore!" Roxy suddenly said, and she took off, looking around at the seaweed, rocks, and coral. Ray swam after her, enjoying the beautiful ocean sights.

Now where did she go? Ray swam to where he thought Roxy was.

"Peek-a-boo!" Roxy suddenly shouted, jumping out from behind a silky fern in the water.

"Aaaahhhhhh!" yelled Ray, momentarily startled, as his eyes got large. He gulped too much water and started coughing.

"Ha!" laughed Roxy, her eyes lit up with playfulness.

Suddenly they were enveloped in a dark, inky fog. As it cleared, they saw Emma, Roxy's friend, the little octopus.

"Sorry I inked, you scared me," Emma explained.

"It's okay, Emma, I understand," Roxy said to her friend.

"Hey, do you remember how you helped heal the suction cups on my arms?" Emma asked.

"Yes," Ray answered, "I remember they were weak. We helped them heal, and you got stronger."

"That's right," Emma answered. "Well, I have a friend who really needs your help now."

"What's wrong?" Roxy asked, concern in her voice.

"My friend Stanley has trouble eating, and he's in pain," Emma explained. "He has a metal hook in his mouth."

"Oh, no!" Roxy gasped, shocked. "I've heard of those, but I never saw one. I wasn't sure they really existed or that something like that could happen."

"Yes, hooks are real. And it's bad," Emma said sadly.

"I'm not sure we can help with that," Ray said.

"But you're Wish Fish, right?" Emma asked.

"Yes, but how could we remove a metal hook?" Ray asked quietly, his voice filled with doubt.

Roxy looked at Ray. "We have to try to help. You always say we can do anything, right?"

Ray hesitated. "I don't know about this, though." His fins drooped. "We do have limits, even if we are Wish Fish. I wouldn't know what to do."

His heart sank. Maybe he had just imagined helping Emma's tentacles. Maybe her arms and suction cups had healed on their own. Maybe it was a coincidence, and he hadn't really helped at all.

Maybe he was even imagining being a Wish Fish. Maybe he was just a small, stupid fish after all, and he couldn't help anyone.

He looked down at his drooping fins. Maybe Roxy was right, and there was no such thing as a Wish Fish. Maybe he was just making a fool of himself.

"Ray," Roxy said softly, moving closer to him. "We might be able to do something, even if we don't know what it is yet. Don't give up. You said we were Wish Fish and that we could do anything."

"But I don't know about this," Ray said sadly.

Emma looked back and forth between them. "Well, at least go and see him. His name is Stanley, and he hangs out by the lagoon over near the coral."

Roxy looked at Ray with hope showing in her eyes. "We have to try," she coaxed.

Ray felt trapped. He didn't want to let down Roxy or Emma, but he couldn't imagine being able to help Stanley. "Okay," he finally muttered, "We can at least see him and take a look."

He looked at Roxy, his fins drooping further. He was filled with self-doubt. This was impossible. He knew that he would disappoint everyone, and then they would all know that he was just a stupid fish and that he couldn't do all those wonderful things.

Maybe he wasn't even a Wish Fish at all. Maybe there was no such thing as a Wish Fish, and he had just imagined the whole thing.

"It will be okay," Roxy told him, touching his face with her soft yellow fin. "We'll just go and see him, that's all. No promises."

Ray let out a big sigh and said nothing.

"Hey Ray, remember what your grandfather told you? That you can do and be anything you wanted?"

"He was just an old senile fish," Ray said quietly.

"No, he was smart. Everyone knew that. And in any case, it won't hurt to just visit Stanley and take a look."

"Okay," Ray said, even though he still didn't think they could help at all. He nodded, and they slowly took off, swimming toward the lagoon near the coral.

❧ CHAPTER 6 ❧
Meeting Stanley

As Ray and Roxy swam closer to the lagoon where Stanley lived, they found seaweed floating out into the water, blocking their view. They swam around some rocks and around the seaweed, and then the water opened up into a beautiful green lagoon.

"Stanley?" Roxy called out.

A skinny, silvery-blue fish came out from behind a fern.

Both Ray and Roxy gasped. Above his skinny body, there was a huge metal hook stuck in his upper lip. They looked up from the hook into Stanley's sad eyes.

"Are you two the Wish Fish that Emma told me about?" Stanley asked, slurring the words around the metal hook in his lip.

"Yes, that's us," Roxy answered. "Emma sent us here to help you."

"I sure hope you can help me. I am so hungry, since it's hard for me to eat. And this hook really hurts. I've tried so many times, but I can't get it out," Stanley told them, as a tear rolled down his sunken cheek.

Ray looked from Stanley to Roxy. *What could they possibly do?* That hook was huge! How could they get it out?

"Believe in yourself," Roxy whispered to Ray. "You're a Wish Fish. You can do this."

Ray looked back at her. "But how? I don't know what to do."

"What was it your grandfather told you about healing?"

"He said that the ocean has healing powers," Ray answered, remembering what he had been told when he was little. "And we can help focus those healing powers where it is needed."

"Good! But first, let's get the hook out."

"How can we do that?"

Roxy turned to Stanley. "How long has this hook been in your lip?"

"A long time," Stanley answered. "It feels like forever."

"Maybe the metal in the hook is weaker by now," she offered.

Ray swam closer. "Well, I know that metal rusts in the ocean water, so that is possible." He touched the hook with a fin, but the hook felt solid.

"Let's focus the healing power of the ocean on Stanley," Roxy suggested.

"Well, it can't hurt," Ray replied.

"What should I do?" Stanley asked them.

"Sit on that rock over there," Ray told him, "and just relax."

Stanley moved over to the rock, let out a big sigh, and relaxed, closing his eyes.

Ray looked at Roxy, a questioning look on his face, and Roxy shrugged.

"We focus healing on Stanley," Ray chanted, not sure if this would work.

"We are healing Stanley," Roxy repeated.

They swam around Stanley, wiggling their fins at him.

"The metal hook is weak," Ray said.

"The metal hook comes out," Roxy added.

They wiggled their fins again at Stanley. They glanced at each other, and suddenly felt a strong vibration in their fins.

Curious, Ray swam closer to Stanley. Looking at the hook, he noticed brown flakes on the metal. *Could that be rust? Was the metal ready to break?*

Feeling renewed, he called to Roxy. "Come help me," he said.

Roxy came over and looked at the hook.

"Look at those brown flakes," Ray said. "I bet that's rust!"

"Maybe we can break the metal now," Roxy said, feeling more hopeful.

"I'll push on this side, and you push on that side," Ray told her. "Maybe we can break it into two pieces."

"I'm not very strong," Roxy told him.

"You're strong enough. Let's try it anyway," Ray said.

Roxy looked at him, suddenly feeling unsure. *Could they really do this?*

❧ CHAPTER 7 ❧
Can He Be Helped?

Ray and Roxy moved to opposite sides of the hook that was in Stanley's lip, and they started pushing.

"Ouch!" cried Stanley. "That hurts!"

"I'm sorry," Roxy told him, quickly moving away.

"Let's help him not feel the pain," Ray suggested.

"You are numb," Roxy chanted to Stanley. "You don't feel anything, your lip is numb, it is cold and numb and you feel nothing. You are relaxed and numb and..."

"...and the metal is weak and soft and it breaks..." added Ray.

"...and you are numb and don't feel it..." continued Roxy.

SNAP! The metal in the hook suddenly cracked, and it now hung in two crooked pieces from his lip. Ray and Roxy jumped in surprise, and Stanley's eyes flew open.

"This is good," Ray said, "now we can pull out the pieces of the hook."

They each grabbed one end of the hook in their mouths and slowly backed up, gently pulling the metal out. As the rusted metal was now soft and broken, it slid out easier than they expected.

Stanley looked at them, eyes brimming over with gratitude. *"You did it! You really did it,"* he cried.

"Wait," Ray told him, "we still need to heal the wound that is left."

They swam closer to Stanley and saw some brown flakes still on his lip. Ray turned around and swished his tail at Stanley, creating a small breezy wave that washed over Stanley's face.

"That's it," cried Roxy. "That's cleaning the rust off him."

"Great," Ray said. "But we still need to help the wound heal."

"That's right," Roxy added. "Let's do the healing again."

They easily fell into their now-familiar routine of chanting healing messages to Stanley.

"Stanley is healthy and strong," Ray chanted.

"Stanley is healthy and strong," Roxy repeated.

They swam around him, wiggling their fins.

Was that enough? Ray wondered what to do next.

"We send glowing light to Stanley," Ray suddenly said, not sure where he had gotten that idea.

Roxy smiled. "We send glowing light to Stanley," she repeated.

They wiggled their fins and swam around the silvery-blue fish. As they completed their circle, they looked at him with disbelief. He was now enveloped in a sphere of glowing light.

They shifted their position in case it was simply an illusion due to the lighting in the water. But wherever they swam and looked at him, there was clearly a bubble of soft, white light around him. *Was that possible?*

"You are healed and happy," Ray chanted, wiggling his fins.

"You are healed and happy," Roxy repeated, wiggling her fins the same way Ray did.

The vibration in their fins felt stronger. *Could they really be doing this?*

They looked back at Stanley and saw that the sphere of light surrounding him was now brighter. He was clearly encircled by a soft, glowing ball of white light. *How was this happening?*

They swam around him one more time, wiggling their fins and chanting words of healing. Then they looked at each other. *Was that it? Were they done?*

They looked at Stanley. He opened his eyes and smiled. "Wow," he said, "I feel better than I have in a long time."

"You're even smiling," Roxy told him.

"Hey, you're right. I could not even do that before."

"Are you okay now?" Roxy asked him.

"Well, I am pretty hungry. I have not been able to eat very well in a long time."

"I wish we had some food for you," Ray said.

"Yes, I wish we had a lot of food to give you," Roxy added.

They felt the movement of a wave through the water, and the three of them turned to look toward the side of the lagoon. There, coming around the corner, was a swirling school of tiny black fish quickly moving toward them. *Food!*

The three of them, their mouths hungrily open, dove toward the tiny black fish, feasting on the delectable bits, eating as much as they could of the yummy morsels until they were full and satisfied.

"Wow," Stanley told them when they were done eating and felt stuffed. "I haven't eaten like that in forever. That was great!"

"Are you feeling better?" Roxy asked him.

"I feel wonderful," Stanley responded, beaming at her. "I feel like a brand new fish! *Thank you!*"

ೞ CHAPTER 8 ೞ
Master Ahi

"That was amazing," Roxy said, as they swam off toward home.

"I know. I'm so glad we really could do something – that felt so good to help him."

"And we have an appointment now," Roxy told him.

"We do?"

"Emma set up a meeting for us with a Master Healer fish."

"A Master Healer fish?" Ray felt confused.

"Yes. Emma said if we really want to continue healing others, we should meet with a Master Healer. She knew one – Master Ahi. And he knew your grandfather."

"Oh, his name is familiar – I remember my grandfather mentioning him."

"His office is over by the reef on the other side."

"Okay, let's head over there," Ray said, his tail swishing back and forth.

"I was excited before, but now I'm scared," Roxy said softly.

"Why? Of what?"

"What if he doesn't like me? What if he thinks I'm stupid? What if I don't understand anything he says?"

"Roxy, you're the smartest and most beautiful fish I've ever met. He will love you."

"I hope so," she whispered.

"Don't worry, Roxy. This will be good for us."

They arrived at the Master's office near the reef, which overlooked some beautiful pink coral. As they swam into the office area, an older brilliant purple fish, with a white face, white fins, and a white tail, came out to greet them.

"Welcome, welcome," he said. "You two must be Ray and Roxy. I am Master Ahi, and I am so happy that you are here. I have heard many good things about you from Emma."

His face lit up with joy, and he held out his fins toward them. Ray thought Master Ahi had the biggest smile he had ever seen on a fish.

"Make yourselves comfortable," Master Ahi told them, gesturing toward some lounging ferns for them to relax on.

They sat down on the soft ferns, feeling a little nervous.

"I understand that you are Wish Fish, and you want to learn more about healing and reaching your full potential. Is that right?"

Both Ray and Roxy nodded, not sure what to expect.

"Excellent! And Ray, I knew your grandfather. He was a very wise fish and a really good friend. I loved him dearly. And you take after him – I can tell that you have many of the same traits as him."

Master Ahi smiled at Ray, and then continued. "I will teach you enough that will get you started on your own journey of growth and healing. You will be able to do amazing things."

The wise purple fish thought for a minute. "First, I would like to show you some points on a fish's body that you can touch to promote healing. For example, here," he said, touching a spot under his fin. "And also here," he added, touching near his tail. "These spots will help stimulate and promote healing, so remember those places."

He gazed joyfully at Ray and Roxy, and then continued. "You can also surround other fish with light – that is also very healing. And somehow I can sense that you already do that – I am impressed."

"Now remember," Master Ahi said, looking at them, "that it's really your intention that directs the energy and holds the most power when you heal and help someone. So always hold love in your heart with the intention of helping the other fish reach their highest good. That makes the healing even stronger. Understand?"

He paused while Ray and Roxy nodded. Then he went on. "And it's important that you be at your best, most pure in heart, and with the highest integrity." He nodded for emphasis.

"And know that all your fears and doubts and difficulties are just opportunities for growth. Okay? Don't let those stop you." Master Ahi smiled at them as they nodded their heads.

"And," he continued, pointing his fin at them to add weight to his words, "remember that you are part of the ocean and everything there is. You are not just in the ocean, but the energy of the ocean is also in you. Feel the power of the ocean, and allow it to move through you. Channel the pure healing energy of the ocean through your body. Then you can more easily send healing love and light to every fish that needs it."

He smiled and made sure Ray and Roxy were both listening. "And remember that you are connected to all other fish, and that you are all one. So what you think and feel will touch and affect everyone and everything around you."

He paused again, letting that sink in, while he sipped some seaweed tea.

"Do you have any questions?" he asked them.

Ray and Roxy shook their heads.

"Now close your eyes and relax," Master Ahi told them, and they closed their eyes. "And now visualize yourselves filled with white light, while I swim around you."

They did as they were told, and they felt the soothing movement of the water around them for a few minutes.

"Excellent, you did wonderful," Master Ahi exclaimed, as they opened their eyes. "You both are very powerful fish. You are indeed Wish Fish, and I'm very impressed."

Ray and Roxy blinked at him, not knowing what to say.

"Before you go," Master Ahi told them, "as you continue your lives in the big wide ocean, always remember three rules that are very important."

"One," he began, pointing with his fin for emphasis, "be thankful for everything in your life. Being grateful helps keep you happy with whatever you have, and it invites even more to come to you."

"Two," he continued, "find joy in your heart, because it is within you, not outside of you."

"And three, always be loving, compassionate, and kind to everything and everyone around you."

He smiled at them as he concluded. "If you follow those rules, you will be happy and at peace, and you will be able to more easily help and heal others as you journey through your life."

Ray and Roxy got off the soft fern and prepared to leave, as the Master put down his cup of tea.

"One last thing," Master Ahi told them, as he showed them to the exit. "And this is important – always believe in yourself. Trust your inner wisdom. You know much more than you think you do." He smiled at them, and then added, "You will do amazing things – much more than I have done, I can promise you that." His smile grew even bigger, his face radiating joy.

"Thank you, Master Ahi," both Ray and Roxy said as they left.

"Wow, that was amazing," Ray told Roxy as they swam toward home.

"I'm not sure I will remember everything he said," Roxy confessed.

"Yeah, me neither. But it sure made a lot of sense while he said it."

"And I had a million questions but couldn't think of what to ask while I was there, because I was so nervous."

"It's okay," Ray told her. "For now, let's just believe in ourselves. I remember that much, at least."

"Okay, I can do that. But I feel exhausted. I think I need a nap now – I'm really tired."

"Yeah, me too," Ray said. "Let's go home and relax."

They slowly swam toward the warm, comfortable water of home, where their eyes closed and they soon drifted off into a wonderful, deep sleep.

✤ CHAPTER 9 ✤
Do Fish Party?

They woke up from their nap feeling refreshed and renewed. They swam in a big, slow, lazy circle around some silky ferns.

"Ray, let's have a party," Roxy said suddenly.

"What? A party? Fish don't have parties," Ray answered.

"But we do lots of things that we thought fish couldn't do. Right? So let's have a party."

Ray looked at Roxy and saw that she was serious. "Okay," he said, wanting to please her. He would do anything to make her happy.

"And let's have it in that little cove around the corner," Roxy added.

"Okay," Ray answered, not sure what he was getting into.

"I'll take care of all the invitations," Roxy said. "And the food," she added.

Ray just nodded, not knowing what to do for a party. He decided to leave it all up to Roxy.

On the day of the party, they headed over to the cove around the corner. Both Ray and Roxy were balancing large trays on their backs.

"What are on these trays?" Ray asked her, as he put his tray down on a flat rock near the side of the cove.

"Crab cookies and tea," Roxy said proudly, as she placed her tray next to the other one.

"Crab cookies? How did you make them?"

"It was easy," laughed Roxy. "I once saw a small crab that had fallen asleep on a rock near the surface of the water. It was in full sun where it was hot, and the crab got baked."

"The crab was cooked?"

"Yes," Roxy said, smiling. "It was delicious! And that gave me the idea for baking crab cookies. Try one," she urged Ray.

Ray reached for a small cookie and put it in his mouth. "Wow, these are delicious," he said with his mouth full.

"Next time I think I will add some kelp chips in them for extra color and flavor," she added.

"And what kind of tea is on the other tray?" Ray asked.

"That's seaweed lemon tea. You will love it," she said.

Once the trays of cookies and tea were set out, they looked around. The cove was clean, there were lots of ferns to relax on, and the decorations of seashells and pink coral were a perfect and festive touch.

"You did a great job getting this place ready," Ray told her.

"Well, thank you for helping to put up the decorations," Roxy answered. "I couldn't do it all by myself."

They looked around and then at each other, hoping their friends would show up.

"Hello? Anyone here?" a small voice called out.

They turned to see Emma the octopus coming into the cove, dragging something behind her.

"Emma," Roxy said, "we are so glad that you came!"

"Look what I can do now," Emma said, as she pulled three round objects in front of her. "You helped heal my tentacles and suction cups, and they are much stronger now. Watch this!" She set around her, in a circle, three empty, round turtle shells.

Emma tapped a few times on the turtle shells with her arms, getting just the right sound and the right beat. Then she began bopping on them, alternating her arms on each of the shells, until she got a good beat going, and all of her arms were joyfully moving with the rhythm.

"After you helped me and I got stronger, I taught myself to play the drums," she said proudly, still drumming. "What do you think?"

"That's wonderful, Emma," Ray exclaimed, as they listened to the engaging rhythm.

"It makes me feel like dancing," Roxy whispered to Ray.

"Is this where the party is?" a small fish voice asked.

They turned to see a little red fish who looked more grown up than she used to. "Bella? Is that you?" Roxy asked.

"It's me!" Bella happily blurted out, as her two bright red parents with black tails followed her into the cove.

"Guess what I can do?" Bella chanted happily. "Watch me!" And she suddenly changed from red to a bright pink with purple polka-dots. "Isn't that cool?" Bella had a big smile on her face.

"She scared us at first," her mom explained. "We thought she was getting sick."

"But she can do this whenever she wants now, and she changes colors all the time," her dad added.

"I like pink and I like polka-dots," Bella stated. "I once saw two yellow fish turn red and blue, and then back to yellow. So I thought that was really cool and that I could try it. Now I can turn any color I want!" she added proudly.

Ray and Roxy glanced at each other. *Had Bella seen the two of them change colors at some time?*

Before Ray or Roxy could answer Bella, a heavy silvery-blue fish entered the cove, carrying a sack of small guppies to snack on. "It's me, Stanley," he said to their confused faces. "And I brought some food for the party."

"Stanley?" Roxy asked, surprised.

"I know, I put on some weight, huh? After you helped me, I realized how skinny and hungry I was. It's been so much fun eating again, that I have been enjoying myself and making up for lost time. And look," he added, sticking out his lip for them to see, "there's barely a scar where that fish hook used to be."

"Wow, you look great, Stanley! Here, put the guppies on this fern where we can snack on them."

As Stanley brought the food to the fern, Ray and Roxy looked at each other. *Wow, this was a better party than they had expected.*

Would anyone else show up?

❧ CHAPTER 10 ❧
The Celebration

An older purple fish with a white face, white fins, and white tail swam into the cove, joining the party. "Hi Ray! Hi Roxy!" he said.

"Master Ahi!" they both answered in unison.

"You have a wonderful party going on here."

As they were about to answer, voices singing got their attention, and they turned to see the four black-and-white seahorses standing behind Emma. The seahorse quartet was singing a song about the sea, singing in perfect four-part harmony, as Emma banged away on the turtle-shell drums.

In front of the music, Bella was happily jumping, swishing, and spinning. She suddenly changed to orange with green polka-dots, and then back to pink with purple polka-dots, as she giggled and snorted. Her parents clapped their fins, both embarrassed and proud of their little girl.

Stanley stayed on the side, stuffing his face with crab cookies, guppies, and the seaweed tea. He stopped for a moment, opened his mouth, and let out a huge belch. He watched the burp bubble rise, and then went back to eating.

"Look around you," Master Ahi told Ray and Roxy. "These are some of the fish that you have helped, whose lives you have touched and changed for the better. These fish are thriving and happy because of you and how you helped them."

Ray and Roxy looked around at Emma, Bella, her parents, Stanley, and the singing seahorses.

"Your small acts of kindness are helping to change everything," he told them. "See how you've already improved so many things by helping these fish. Each act of kindness, no matter how small, helps to change the whole world. And you will do much more, too."

Master Ahi looked at them. "I am so very proud of both of you," he said smiling. Then he glided over to the crab cookies, before they were all eaten by Stanley.

Ray clapped his fins to get everyone's attention. "We want to thank all of you for coming to our party," he told everyone. "This party is really a celebration. We are celebrating the gift of friendship that each of you has given us. And we want to tell you how thankful and grateful we are that you are part of our lives."

"And thank you for trusting us and allowing us to help you," Roxy added.

"And for adding such joy to our lives," Ray said.

"And we also want to celebrate our love," Roxy added. "Not just between the two of us, but from both of us to all of you!"

Everyone cheered and clapped, wiggling their fins enthusiastically. Off to the side, they saw Master Ahi raise a cup of tea toward them as a toast. He drank it and then winked at them, a huge smile on his face.

Within a few minutes, the seahorses resumed singing, Emma went back to banging on the turtle-shell drums, Bella spun in circles, and Stanley gulped down more guppies and crab cookies. Master Ahi laughed joyfully and sipped at some tea.

What a great party this was! This must be the best fish party ever!

❧ CHAPTER 11 ❧
Endless Possibilities

After taking down the decorations and cleaning up from the party, Ray and Roxy spent a whole day just resting and being lazy. They swam through the ferns and took an extra nap in the afternoon.

"What now, Ray? We've discovered the secret of being a Wish Fish. We've learned how to heal. And we can do amazing things – things that I never thought were possible. So what more is there? What else can we do?"

"The possibilities are endless, Roxy. Even *we* don't know."

"Then how do we know what to try next?"

"Use your imagination," Ray suggested. "What gets you excited? What makes you feel good and come alive? What do you want more of?"

Roxy hesitated. "Don't laugh at me," she finally said.

"What is it, Roxy?"

"Promise you won't laugh?"

"Yes, of course, I promise."

Roxy smiled at him. "Dancing," she admitted.

"*Dancing?* You told me fish can't dance."

"Yeah, I know. But it was really fun. It made me feel happy, like nothing else existed. Like I was just pure liquid joy."

"I'm glad you liked that. I actually liked it, too," Ray said smiling. "Would you like to try dancing with me now?"

"Well, we can dance, as long as you don't sing," Roxy answered, snickering.

"Okay, it's a deal. I won't sing. I promise. I'll leave that to the seahorses."

They reached their fins toward each other, and Roxy gracefully twirled around a few times.

"Wow – Roxy, you got better! You are good!"

"I practiced a lot when you weren't looking. I was even thinking of opening a dance studio and maybe teaching other fish to dance."

"Really? That is wonderful – you'd be great, Roxy!"

"I especially love the Wish-Fish Cha-Cha," she laughed. "And maybe little Bella can be my first student. She was great at our party."

"As long as none of your students will become invisible and hard to see," Ray smirked.

Roxy giggled, and bubbles rose from her nose.

"Wow, who would have ever thought we could do what we've done," she said.

"You're right," Ray agreed. "We changed color and also became invisible."

"And we glowed, too," Roxy added.

"And we healed other fish and surrounded them with light."

"And we flew – *can you believe that one?*" Roxy said, astonished.

"And we danced," Ray said, twirling his fins.

"We can do *anything*," Roxy said happily. "Including throwing the best party."

"We're Wish Fish," Ray stated, as though that explained it all.

"Yes," Roxy nodded her head. "And we are the best Wish Fish *ever!*"

"And we can do the Wish-Fish Cha-Cha," Ray said, laughing.

Roxy giggled. "And we're also in love."

"That's the *best* part," Ray stated.

"And the *other* best part," Roxy said with excitement, "is that we really can help other fish. I love that."

"Yup. And the *other* best part is that we don't even know what else we can do. There must be a million, billion, *gazillion* new things we could do, and we don't even know it yet."

"Infinite possibilities," Roxy said.

"Yes," Ray agreed. "Endless possibilities."

"And we're just getting started," Roxy smiled at him.

"And then we can teach other fish to do what we can do," Ray said.

"They will be able to do even *more* than we can," Roxy added.

"I love you more than anything in the whole ocean," Ray said, looking into Roxy's beautiful eyes.

"I love you more than anything in the whole world," Roxy answered him.

They touched each other's fins, while Roxy twirled around, and they did a few more steps of the Wish-Fish Cha-Cha. Roxy wiggled her hips, and they giggled like silly little fish, as bubbles rose in the warm water.

Together, they swam in circles around the ferns, as joy filled their hearts to overflowing.

There was nothing better in the whole world than being a Wish Fish.

And the possibilities were truly endless.

ABOUT THE AUTHOR

LYNN MICLEA is a writer, author, musician, Reiki master practitioner, and dog lover.

Although she worked many different jobs throughout her life, she has always loved reading and writing, and one of her dreams was to become a professional writer.

After retiring, Lynn further pursued her passion for writing, and she is now a successful author with many books published and more on the way.

She has published books of fiction (thrillers, suspense, romance, science fiction, paranormal, and mystery), nonfiction (memoirs and self-help guided imagery), and children's stories (fun animal stories about kindness, believing in yourself, helping others, and being more than you ever thought possible).

She hopes that through her writing she can help empower others, stimulate people's imagination, and open new worlds as she entertains with powerful and heartfelt stories.

Originally from New York, Lynn currently lives in southern California with her loving and supportive husband.

Please visit *www.lynnmiclea.com* for more information.

BOOKS BY LYNN MICLEA

Fiction
New Contact
Transmutation
Journey Into Love
Ghostly Love
Guard Duty
Loving Guidance
The Diamond Murders
The Sticky-Note Murders

Non-Fiction
Ruthie: A Family's Struggle with ALS
Mending a Heart: A Journey Through Open-Heart Surgery
Unleash Your Inner Joy – Volume 1: Peace
Unleash Your Inner Joy – Volume 2: Abundance
Unleash Your Inner Joy – Volume 3: Healing
Unleash Your Inner Joy – Volume 4: Spirituality

Children's Books
Penny Gains Confidence
Sammy and the Fire
Sammy Visits a Hospital
Sammy Meets Grandma
Sammy Goes to the Dog Park
Sammy Falls in Love
Sammy and the Earthquake
Sammy Goes On Vacation
Wish Fish: Book 1 – Discovering the Secret
Wish Fish: Book 2 – Endless Possibilities

ONE LAST THING...

Thank you for reading this book — you are *awesome!*

If you enjoyed this book, I'd be very grateful if you would post a short review on Amazon. Your support really makes a big difference and helps me immensely!

Simply click the "leave-a-review" link for this book at Amazon, and leave a short review. It would mean a lot to me!

Thank you so much for your support—it is very appreciated!

Thank You!

Printed in Great Britain
by Amazon

31143527R00046